Looking after God's World

by
Karen Holford

Illustrated by Chiara Vercesi

Daddy picked up Tim's blue bucket and filled it right up to the top with sand that was just a little bit wet. He patted the sand with the flat part of the yellow spade until the sand was hard and smooth.

Then he held his hand over the sand in the bucket and carefully turned it upside down onto the beach. He tapped the bucket gently and then lifted it up slowly and carefully. A perfect little sandcastle sat on the beach. Susie found some seashells and daddy used them to make windows and doors for the tiny castle.

Tim tried to make a sandcastle. He filled his bucket with sand and quickly turned it upside down, but all he made was a mess!

He watched daddy make another castle with Susie's bucket. Tim filled his bucket with sand again, pressed it down hard with his hands and his spade, and daddy turned it upside down for him. This time the castle looked almost perfect.

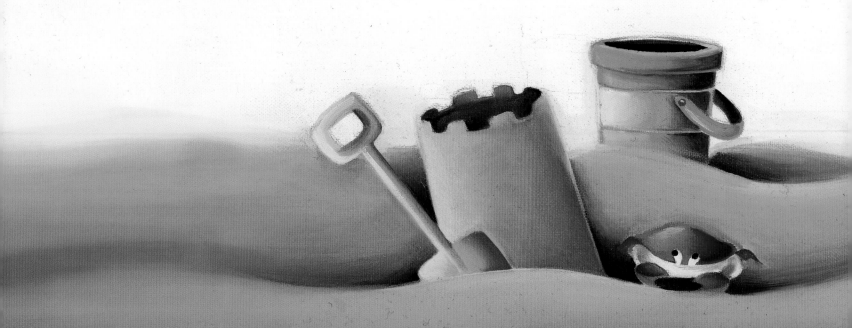

Susie put some shells on the castle to make some windows, but she pressed too hard and the castle fell down again.

'Never mind,' said daddy, 'I've got an idea. Let's build a really big castle. Fill up your buckets with sand and empty them inside this circle, and we'll make the best sandcastle ever!'

Susie and Tim filled their buckets with sand as quickly as they could and emptied them inside the big circle that daddy had drawn on the beach.

Daddy patted the sand with his hands until it was hard. The castle grew higher and higher. It was hard work, but it was fun.

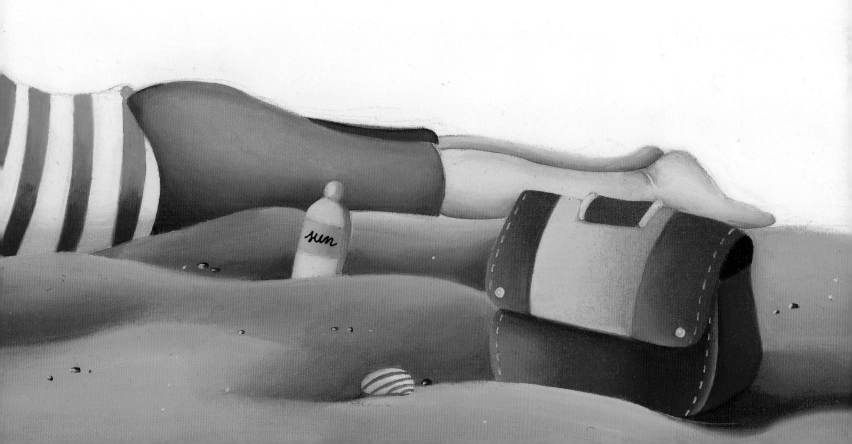

Then daddy made some tall towers for the top of the castle. Mummy collected seashells and helped them to decorate the walls. Tim pressed a piece of smooth wood onto the front of the castle to make a door.

They dug a ditch all around the castle. Daddy called it a moat and said it was to stop bad people getting inside.

They tried to fill it with water from the sea, but the water disappeared into the sand. So they filled the moat with wet, green seaweed and pretended it was water.

It was hard work, digging and building. But when they had finished they all agreed it was the best sandcastle they had ever seen.

At lunchtime they ran into the edge of the cold sea and washed their hands. They ate their sandwiches, crisps, carrot sticks, fruit cake and apples. Seagulls came to watch them eat.

They seemed to scream for food, so Tim threw them some crumbs.

When they'd finished eating, daddy collected up all the rubbish and put it into an old plastic bag. An empty crisp packet blew away along the beach and daddy ran after it. He didn't want to spoil the beach with even the tiniest bit of litter.

After lunch mummy read her book, and daddy, Susie and Tim walked along the beach to the little ice-cream shop by the harbour. Next to the harbour stood a row of big bins on wheels for all the rubbish from the boats, so daddy took the bag of lunch litter with him.

After daddy had thrown their rubbish safely into one of the bins, they went to buy their ice-creams. Tim chose chocolate ice-cream, Susie wanted strawberry ripple, and daddy bought a newspaper to read. They sat on a bench, eating their ice-creams and watching sailing boats and seagulls.

Then they walked back to their castle, paddling in the white, lacy waves along the edge of the sea.

Suddenly Tim started to run. 'Oh, no!' he said. Daddy looked up and saw that their castle had been squashed.

The highest tower had fallen into the moat, the walls had been flattened, and shells and seaweed were all mixed up in the sand. Susie began to cry.

A man came over to them and said, 'Is this your castle?' Tim nodded sadly.

'I'm so sorry,' said the man. 'My dog Bobby was running along the beach after his ball and he didn't look where he was going, so he ran right through your lovely castle. I couldn't stop him in time.'

'It's OK,' said daddy, 'we'll make a new one.'

mouth
10 August

'Well, I've got a big bucket here,' said the man. 'I'll help to get you started. You know, it's been a long time since I made a sandcastle! I'm a builder, so we should have a brand new castle in no time at all!'

He was right. Soon the castle was bigger and better than ever before, with new towers and strong walls. Mummy helped them to find more shells to decorate the walls. Daddy took a picture of Susie and Tim next to their amazing sandcastle and soon it was time to go back to their holiday caravan.

At bedtime they read the story of Creation because it was Susie's favourite. She loved hearing about all the animals God made. Then they went through the alphabet, thinking of lots of lovely things that God had made.

Air. Beaches. Cats. Chocolate. . . . By the time they reached 'S' there were so many things on their list! They added Susie. Sand. Seagulls. When they reached the end of the alphabet Tim said, 'Hey, I know what we missed out! Ice-cream!' And they all laughed.

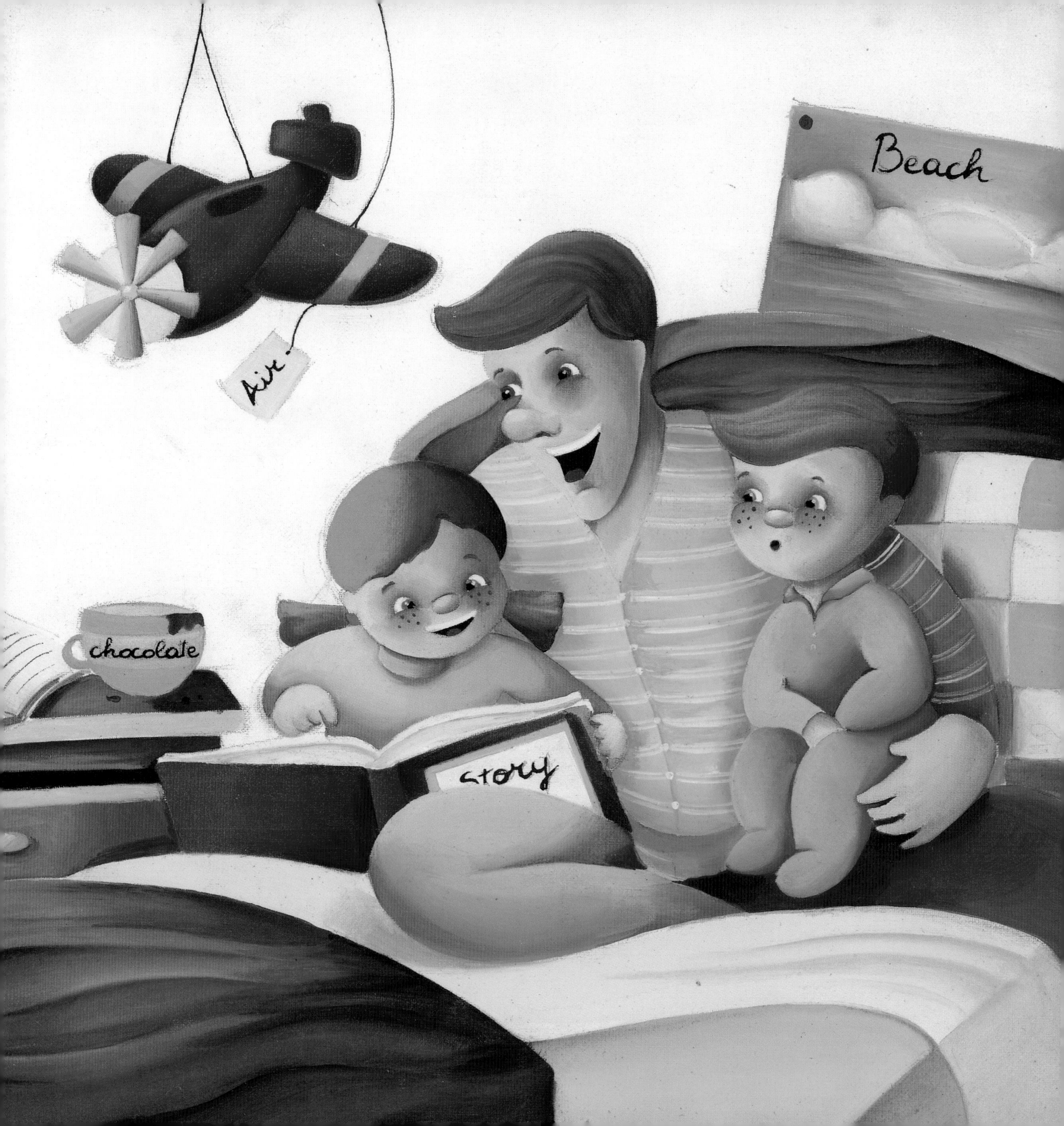
Beach
Air
chocolate
story

That night the wind blew loud and strong. Things bumped and crashed in the night, and the caravan shook. But they were all safe inside.

In the morning mummy packed another picnic and they drove to the beach as soon as they were ready. Susie ran onto the beach. Then she stopped and said, 'What happened to our lovely beach? It looks horrible!'

'Oh, dear,' said daddy, who was just behind her, 'I think the storm must have blown over one of the big bins by the harbour.' Bits of newspaper, plastic bags, empty bottles, lolly wrappers, tin cans and broken spades were all over the sand.

Tim said, 'Let's go to a nice beach. I don't want to play here.'

But mummy had a different idea. 'I know, why don't we help to make this beach better again? Someone needs to pick everything up and make it clean. If all of this washes out to sea it will spoil other beaches and maybe hurt the fish, too.'

'You're right,' said daddy. 'We've got a roll of bin bags in the car and we could fill them with all the rubbish right here. Someone needs to do the job and it might as well be us. Our rubbish from yesterday is probably blowing around, too. When God made the world he gave people the job of taking care of everything. So when we find a mess, it's important for us to help clean it up. It's our way of saying "thank you" to God for all the amazing things he's made. Remember, yesterday we built a lovely castle and we were so sad when Bobby crashed into it and broke it down? I think God must feel a bit like that when people do things that spoil his lovely world. It was kind of Bobby's owner to come and help us fix the castle again. That made us feel good, didn't it? I think God would be really happy to see us clean up this mess.'

Susie and Tim didn't think picking up rubbish would be fun. They thought they would much rather build a sandcastle. So mummy said, 'Let's have a race! Susie can help me and Tim can help daddy, and we'll see who can fill the most bags in half an hour! Then we'll go down to the little shop and the winning team can have a chocolate flake in their ice-cream!'

Mummy told the children to be careful what they picked up so they wouldn't hurt themselves. She found thick plastic bags, wrapped them around their hands and tied the handles around their wrists. They could still pick things up, but it would be safer for their hands. Mummy and daddy picked up anything sharp or dirty.

They soon filled their bags. There were lots of plastic bottles and newspapers. Susie found a bucket with a broken handle that would help them make a new sandcastle, and Tim found a flag to go on the top.

Another family came down to the beach and asked if they could help, too. It wasn't long before the beach looked even better than before! Soon there was no litter to be found anywhere. Some men helped daddy to turn the big bin by the harbour the right way up again, and they filled it with all of their rubbish bags.

When they went into the ice-cream shop the lady said, 'Thank you for tidying up! That was so kind of you! When I saw the mess I thought no one would want to come today and I wouldn't be able to sell many ice-creams, but you've all done a lovely job! I want you to have a free ice-cream. You can choose anything you like. You can even have three scoops, and a chocolate flake, if you want to!'

They sat down by the harbour to eat their huge ice-creams. Each of them had a chocolate flake in their cone. Tim ate his chocolate flake first, and Susie pushed hers right down inside the ice-cream to save it till last.

They looked at all the children playing on the beautiful beach. Then Tim said, 'I'm glad we tidied everything up. It was more fun than I thought it would be. Everything looks so much nicer now! I'm sure God was happy we helped, too.'

'I'm sure he was!' said daddy, standing up. 'Now, who's ready to build the biggest sandcastle in the whole wide world?'

First published in 2010
Copyright © 2010 Autumn House Publishing (Europe) Ltd.

Author: Karen Holford

Illustrator: Chiara Vercesi

British Library Cataloguing in Publication Data.
A catalogue record for this book is available from the British Library.

ISBN 978-1-906381-95-0

Published by Autumn House, Alma Park, Grantham, Lincs.

Printed in China.